Samuel French Acting Edition

Onegin

by Amiel Gladstone
& Veda Hille

SAMUELFRENCH.COM   SAMUELFRENCH.CO.UK

FOR PRODUCTION ENQUIRIES

UNITED STATES AND CANADA
Info@SamuelFrench.com
1-866-598-8449

UNITED KINGDOM AND EUROPE
Plays@SamuelFrench.co.uk
020-7255-4302

Each title is subject to availability from Samuel French, depending upon country of performance. Please be aware that *ONEGIN* may not be licensed by Samuel French in your territory. Professional and amateur producers should contact the nearest Samuel French office or licensing partner to verify availability.

MUSIC USE NOTE

Licensees are solely responsible for obtaining formal written permission from copyright owners to use copyrighted music in the performance of this play and are strongly cautioned to do so. If no such permission is obtained by the licensee, then the licensee must use only original music that the licensee owns and controls. Licensees are solely responsible and liable for all music clearances and shall indemnify the copyright owners of the play(s) and their licensing agent, Samuel French, against any costs, expenses, losses and liabilities arising from the use of music by licensees. Please contact the appropriate music licensing authority in your territory for the rights to any incidental music.

IMPORTANT BILLING AND CREDIT REQUIREMENTS

If you have obtained performance rights to this title, please refer to your licensing agreement for important billing and credit requirements.

ONEGIN is based on the poem by Pushkin and the opera by Tchaikovsky.

ONEGIN was commissioned by Arts Club Theatre Company and premiered in March 2016. The performance was directed by Amiel Gladstone, with musical direction by Veda Hille, set design by Drew Facey, costume design by Jacqueline Firkins, lighting design by John Webber, sound design by Bradley Danyluk, and choreography by Tracey Power. The stage manager was Allison Spearin, and the dramaturg was Rachel Ditor. The cast was as follows:

TATYANA LARIN . . . . .Meg Roe

EVGENI ONEGIN. . . . . Alessandro Juliani

VLADIMIR LENSKY. . . . . Josh Epstein

OLGA LARIN & OTHERS. . . . . Lauren Jackson

MADAME LARIN & OTHERS. . . . . Caitriona Murphy

PRINCE GREMIN & OTHERS . . . . Andrew Wheeler

MANY OTHERS . . . . .Andrew McNee

THE UNGRATEFUL DEAD. . . . . Veda Hille
Barry Mirochnick
Marina Hasselberg

Additional development at Musical Stage Company, Toronto; production May 2017.

The U.S. premiere of *ONEGIN* took place at Greater Boston Stage Company in March 2019.

CHARACTERS

VLADIMIR LENSKY
EVGENI ONEGIN
TATYANA LARIN
OLGA LARIN
MADAME LARIN
TRIQUET
ZARETSKY
GUILLOT
PRINCE GREMIN
ENSEMBLE, GOSSIPS, PARTYGOERS

SETTING

Various houses and rooms in the country and city of nineteenth-century
Russia, mixed with modern-day. A big wood floor. Lots of light. Books
everywhere. Common theatre gak like lighting instruments, cables,
microphones, ropes, and rugs.

The performers move throughout the audience. Scenes move fluidly
from place to place.

TIME

An imaginary 1819, then six years later.

AUTHOR'S NOTES

Pronunciations
It's very challenging to get the correct Russian in English, so forgive us
our approximations. We have settled on:
Onegin: ah-NYAY-gin
Larin: LAH-rin
Lubov: LU-boif
Neva: NYAY-vah

Doubling
If you've got seven actors (the minimum) then this works: Tatyana,
Onegin, and Lensky only play themselves. Olga also plays Woman 1 and
Ensemble. Madame Larin also plays Zaretsky, Woman 2, and Ensemble.

Triquet also plays Ensemble, Another Man, and Guillot. Prince Gremin also plays the dying Uncle, A Man, and Ensemble. Sometimes it's like the Ensemble members individually are each representing a group of people at a party.

Style

Flipping between concert and full-scale opera. Big emotions that feel real, and at the same time a theatrical awareness of story and spectacle. We found that including the audience as much as possible was the way to go. Get out there when you can to sit with them, be present with them. The ad-lib conversations off the top should be genuine and fun, and never rushed. Those conversations are a real opportunity to show how much you love the audience, how glad you are they came, and to start talking about the themes.

Smarts

Part of the key is that we always need to show how smart and ahead of her time Tatyana is. She's always the smartest in the room. So make choices that are strong-willed and give her agency (as much as she can in the confines of all that patriarchy, anyway). So Onegin has to be careful – if he's too much of a dick to her, she looks dumb for falling for him. We have to see what's great about him, who he'd be if he wasn't so screwed up by loss of parents, money, etc. Allow her to make great choices – Onegin is definitely flawed, but we need to see his sexy good qualities.

And then Gremin should be a great choice for her too. He's older, sure, but still dashing, and he takes care of her and makes her happy – they have an adoring marriage so far.

Emotion

We erred on the side of love, spreading it around as much as possible and making sure the audience felt a part of it all.

ACKNOWLEDGEMENTS

Thanks to the Arts Club Theatre Company and their Re:Act play development program and all the generous staff there, especially to Rachel Ditor for championing from early days.

So many talented folks helped us along the way, apologies for omissions.

InTune Conference, Touchstone Theatre, PL1422, Playwrights Guild of Canada, Pechet Family, Vancouver Opera, Mitchell Marcus, Michael Shamata, On Egin in Berlin, Sarah May Redmond, Warren Kimmel, Cameron McPhail, Naomi Campbell, Igor Rozenberg, Deborah Vogt, David McIntosh, Bill Richardson, Gary Cristall, Jillian Keiley, Nathan Medd, and the staff at the NAC.

Our MDs: Chris Tsujiuchi, Margeurite Witvoet, Steve Bass.

Our copyists: Kevin Wong, Mary Jane Paquette, Deanna Choi.

Josh Epstein, Alessandro Juliani, Meg Roe, Andrew McNee, Lauren Jackson, Andrew Wheeler, Caitriona Murphy, Barry Mirochnick, Marina Hasselberg, Meaghan Chenosky, Erik Fraser Gow, Nadeem Phillip, Jonathan Winsby, Allison Spearin, Sandra Drag, Jennifer Moersch, Tracey Power, John Webber, Drew Facey, Jacqueline Firkins, Bradley Danyluk, and everyone at the Arts Club under Bill Millerd's artistic direction.

Mitchell Marcus, Paul Beauchamp, Hailey Gillis, Daren Herbert, Peter Fernandes, Shane Carty, Elena Juatco, Rebecca Auerbach, AJ Laflamme, Erika Nielsen, Denyse Karn, Michael Laird, Anna Treusch, Oz Weaver, Linda Garneau, and everyone at Musical Stage Company.

Weylin Symes, Ilyse Robbin, Peter Adams, Christopher Chew, Kerry Dowling, Josephine Moshiri Elwood, Mark Linehan, Michael Jennings Mahoney, Sarah Pothier, Deirdre Benson, and the entire Greater Boston Stage Company team.

Amy Lynn Strilchuk! Justin Kellam! Anders Kellam!

And of course, Aleksándr Sergéyevich and Pyótr Il'yích.

SONG LIST

ACT ONE

Scene One

(During the curtain speech telling people to turn off cell phones, forbidding use of recording devices, thanking sponsors, etc. the cast and band take the stage, seeming to come from everywhere.)

[MUSIC NO. 01 "A LOVE SONG"]

LENSKY.

A LOVE SONG WE SING TO YOU,
WE BEG THAT YOU MIGHT HEAR IT

MADAME LARIN.

OH HOW WE LOVE TO DREAM OF LOVE,
INVITING PUSHKIN'S SPIRIT

ONEGIN.

UNTETHER NOW, FROM DAY TO DAY,
WHERE LOVE MAY REMAIN UNSPOKEN

TATYANA.

WE HOPE TO PLEASE,
WE HOPE TO CHARM, WE HOPE TO BREAK YOU OPEN.

A MAN.

THE ARCHER LETS AN ARROW FLY: WILL IT FIND ITS
MARK?

ALL.

ONCE WE MAKE LOVE IS IT HERE TO STAY?

ANOTHER MAN.

FOR WHERE IT LANDS

MADAME LARIN.

AND HOW IT ENDS

TATYANA.

AND WHO WILL LIVE IN LOVE

ONEGIN.

WELL, THAT IS HARD TO SAY...

(A loud crack! And an instant tableau: **TATYANA** *kneeling in the snow between* **ONEGIN** *and* **LENSKY** *with pistols.)*

[MUSIC NO. 02 "OH DEAR FATHER"]

TATYANA.	**ENSEMBLE.**
OH DEAR FATHER UP IN HEAVEN	OOO
RELEASE US FROM BOREDOM	
OH DEAR FATHER UP IN HEAVEN	OOO
SEND US A GOOD TIME	
OH DEAR FATHER UP IN HEAVEN	AAH
LOOK DOWN AT US SMILING	
OH DEAR FATHER MAKE IT HAPPEN	AAH
TONIGHT!	

(The party kicks in. Chandeliers and candles. Dancing and drinking.)

(An ensemble looking to have a good time.)

A MAN. *(At a microphone.)* Ladies and gentlemen – and everybody else!

Let me introduce

A young poet for our time!

*(***LENSKY*** *takes the mic.)*

LENSKY.

MY NAME IS VLADIMIR LENSKY

I'M SURE YOU HAVE HEARD OF ME

I'M A POET, IN RUSSIA, IN THE NINETEENTH CENTURY

THAT'S RIGHT, THAT'S RIGHT, THAT'S RIGHT

I'M A ROMANTIC!

OLGA. Just like our dear author Alexander Pushkin. He wrote the poem on which tonight's performance is based.

MADAME LARIN. Russia's greatest writer, and quite a lover as well.

LENSKY. He and I have much in common.

> *(A sting from the drummer and scoffing laughter all around.)*

A MAN. Pushkin was killed in a duel. His twenty-ninth duel.

ALL.

> *AN INSULT! LEADS TO A CHALLENGE! LEADS TO AGREEMENT!*
> *LEADS TO A RENDEZVOUS!*

LENSKY. Twenty paces leads to a shot!

ANOTHER MAN. Only thirty-seven years old, but Pushkin died for honour.

ALL.

> HONOUR!

LENSKY.

> NOW THAT IS WORTH DEATH!
> AND THAT IS THE TRUTH
> HONOUR AND LOVE, HONOUR AND LOVE

ALL.

> LOVE!

MADAME LARIN.

> *IN RUSSIAN:*
> *LUBOV.*

LENSKY & OLGA.

> LOOK AROUND, LOOK AROUND, LOOK AROUND
> DO YOU SEE SOMEONE WORTH DYING FOR?

> *(**LENSKY** heads into the audience.)*

LENSKY. *(Picking a specific target in the audience.)* That's right I'm talking to you.

(Ad-lib.) Yes, that's right. No fourth wall. We couldn't afford it. *[Etc.]* So. Tell me. Do you see someone worth dying for? Here, tonight? Who? *[Etc.]*

Thank you for coming!

ALL.

> LOOK AROUND, LOOK AROUND, LOOK AROUND

LENSKY.

> DO YOU SEE SOMEONE WORTH DYING FOR?
> THAT'S RIGHT, THAT'S RIGHT, THAT'S RIGHT
> I'M A ROMANTIC!

ANOTHER MAN. So here we all are. You all look divine.

> *(Picking specific targets,* **LENSKY** *joins him.)* Especially you two over here.
>
> *(Ad-lib.)* Are you on a date? Do you want it to be a date? Where did you meet? Tinder? *[Etc.]*
>
> Are you in love? Yes? No?

LENSKY. *(Ad-lib.)* Who loves each other more? You? You?

OLGA. Welcome! We are glad you are here.

A MAN. It's 1819. Give or take.

MADAME LARIN. Saint Petersburg. Give or take. And west, at the Larin estate.

OLGA. It's Russia. It's late summer. It's a long time ago.

ANOTHER MAN. It feels like the entire town is crammed in here.

LENSKY. I propose: a drinking game.

> In order to help tonight go down a little easier – and for you to forgive the moments when we all get too carried away. So. Every time someone says the word "love" in Russian, "lubov," we drink!

ALL. Lubov!

> *(All drink.)*

LENSKY. Get me another!

ALL.

> SAINT PETER WILL ASK YOU WHEN YOU GET TO HEAVEN'S DOOR
> WHATEVER DID YOU DO DOWN THERE TO KEEP FROM BEING BORED?
> WHAT DID YOU DO FOR, WHO DID YOU DO FOR...

LENSKY.

> *L'AMOUR!*

(Everyone is disappointed that they can't drink.)

ALL.

SAINT PETER WILL ASK YOU WHEN YOU GET TO HEAVEN'S DOOR
WHATEVER DID YOU DO DOWN THERE TO KEEP FROM BEING BORED?
WHAT DID YOU DO FOR, WHO DID YOU DO FOR...

LENSKY.

LUBOV!

(All drink.)

All right! Now you are getting into the right frame of mind.

A MAN. And now I'd like to introduce the most talented people on the stage: our band!

ANOTHER MAN. The Ungrateful Dead.

(Each member of the band does a short, showy solo, and **A MAN** *announces their names:)*

A MAN. On cello, [*name of musician*]! On drums, [*name of musician*]! On piano, [*name of musician*]!

ALL.

THE BAND IS GOOD
THE DRINK IS STRONG
DANCE A LITTLE HARDER,
DANCE A LITTLE LONG –
GIRRRLS!

*(***OLGA** *and* **TATYANA** *dance.)*

BOYS!

*(***LENSKY** *and* **ANOTHER MAN** *dance.)*

OLD MEN AND MOTHERS TOO.

*(***A MAN** *and* **MADAME LARIN** *struggle to dance, briefly.)*

JUST THROW YOURSELVES TOGETHER AND DO LIKE PEOPLE SHOULD
DO, LIKE PEOPLE SHOULD DO!

(Everyone dances.)

ALL.

OH DEAR FATHER UP IN HEAVEN
RELEASE US FROM BOREDOM
OH DEAR FATHER UP IN HEAVEN

SEND US A GOOD TIME
OH DEAR FATHER UP IN HEAVEN
LOOK DOWN AT US SMILING
OH DEAR FATHER MAKE IT HAPPEN
MAKE IT HAPPEN
OH DEAR FATHER UP IN HEAVEN
RELEASE US FROM BOREDOM
OH DEAR FATHER UP IN HEAVEN
LET THIS PLAY BE GOOD!
GODDAMN BE GOOD, GODDAMN BE GOOD, GODDAMN BE GOOD. GODDAMN!

(They all talk about the last horrible play they saw. And then the tune kicks back in.)

WOMEN.	**MEN.**
WE HOPE TO PLEASE	SAINT PETER WILL ASK YOU WHEN YOU GET
WE HOPE TO CHARM	TO HEAVEN'S DOOR
WE HOPE TO BREAK YOU	WHATEVER DID YOU DO DOWN THERE TO
OPEN	KEEP FROM BEING BORED?
UNTETHER NOW FROM DAY TO DAY	WHAT DID YOU DO FOR
WHERE LOVE REMAINS UNSPOKEN	WHO DID YOU DO FOR LOVE LOVE LOVE

ALL.

A LOVE SONG I SING TO YOU
A LOVE SONG I SING TO YOU

WOMEN.	**MEN.**
OH DEAR FATHER UP IN HEAVEN	IT'S RUSSIA! LATE SUMMER! IT'S A LONG TIME AGO!

RELEASE US FROM
   BOREDOM

OH DEAR FATHER UP IN
   HEAVEN

LET
THIS
PLAY
BE
GOOD!

WHATEVER DID YOU DO
   DOWN THERE TO KEEP
   FROM BEING BORED?
IT'S RUSSIA! LATE
   SUMMER!
IT'S A LONG TIME AGO!
WHAT DID YOU
WHAT DID YOU
WHAT DID YOU
DO FOR
LOVE?

LENSKY. Are we ready?

ALL. Yes!

LENSKY. And now we present:

ALL.

EVGENI ONEGIN!

(And there, suddenly, dressed impeccably, is the man himself, **ONEGIN**.*)*

(Shift.)

Scene Two

[MUSIC NO. 03 "THREE HORSES"]

(**ONEGIN** *in a carriage.*)

ONEGIN.

THREE HORSES
WINTER'S HEAVY SNOW
DOES THIS SEEM FAMILIAR?
A PLACE, A PERSON YOU MIGHT KNOW?
HERE ARE THE FACTS AT HAND:
A CHARMING RAKISH YOUNG DANDY IS WHO I AM.

THREE HORSES
BIRCH TREES, SNOW
YOU'VE SEEN THIS BEFORE.
AM I A PERSON YOU WANT TO KNOW?
WELL TRAVELLED AND WEALTHY
ALWAYS IN FASHION, ALWAYS SO MELANCHOLY.

BORN IN SAINT PETERSBURG, A CITY BUILT
ON VANITY AND SILT   **CHORUS.**
BY THE PEOPLE'S LABOUR   PEOPLE'S LABOUR
BESIDE THE RIVER NEVA   RIVER NEVA
A TOAST, A TOAST
WE ARE GHOSTS UPON GHOSTS UPON GHOSTS
BONNE SOIRÉE, MA CHERIE, JE T'ADORE
YOU DON'T CARE, YOU DON'T CARE, YOU DON'T CARE

> (*He leaps into the audience. Finds a woman.
> Or several.*)

(*Ad-lib.*) Wow. You really don't care. I love it.
Come backstage after the show and we can "not care"
together.

> (*He leaps back onstage.*)

SURPRISE ME, AMUSE ME, SHAKE ME
I DARE YOU TRY
TRY TO WAKE ME

> (*His* **UNCLE** *appears on his deathbed.*)

I GO TO SEE MY UNCLE
HE ISN'T WELL
HE IS DYING
AS WE ALL WILL
AS MY PARENTS DID
I BURIED THEM.
I TAKE CARE OF MYSELF

AS YOU SHOULD, AS YOU SHOULD, AS YOU SHOULD

    (His **UNCLE** *dies.)*

TO YOUR HEALTH!
A TOAST, A TOAST
WE ARE GHOSTS UPON GHOSTS UPON GHOSTS
I DO AS I LIKE, AS I DARE
YOU DON'T CARE, YOU DON'T CARE, YOU DON'T CARE

THREE HORSES
CANTER THROUGH THE SNOW
HERE WE ARE AGAIN
DO YOU KNOW ME? DO YOU WANT TO KNOW?
HERE ARE THE FACTS AT HAND:

EVGENI ONEGIN IS WHO I AM!

    *(***ONEGIN** *has arrived at the country estate.*
    LENSKY *throws him a rifle.)*

LENSKY. Ah, is there anything more bracing than a shooting party in the autumnal air!

ONEGIN. A party? There's just two of us.

LENSKY. My friend, with you it is a party! Even when you're grief-stricken. Although with your aim it looks like your supper will be light tonight.

ONEGIN. You just wait until the winter dances begin.

LENSKY. Oh I see.

ONEGIN. There you will see me hit my mark.

LENSKY. Well then, we shall have to make your introductions. People are starting to talk.

ONEGIN. Small town, small talk. What do I care?

    *(***LENSKY** *slaps* **ONEGIN***'s chest three times.)*

LENSKY.

>OH, DON'T WASTE YOUR LIFE: COME DOWN! JOIN US ON
>　　THE GROUND!

I am calling on the Larin estate this afternoon, come with me! You still haven't met my Olga.

>I WOULD DIE FOR HER!

ONEGIN. You've been dying for her constantly the entire time I have known you.

LENSKY. *(Quoting.)* "The light of love, the purity of grace,
The mind, the Music breathing from her face,
The heart whose softness harmonised the whole –
And, oh! that eye was in itself a Soul!"

ONEGIN. Please keep your Byron to yourself.

LENSKY. *(Exiting.)* My Olga has a sister...

CHORUS.

>TATYANA!

ONEGIN.

>HERE ARE THE FACTS AT HAND: EVGENI ONEGIN IS WHO
>　　I AM!

CHORUS.

>HIS SUITS ARE FROM PARIS
>AHEAD OF THE FASHION
>HIS FRENCH IS FLAWLESS
>HE KNOWS HIS BYRON
>THE CATCH OF THE CENT'RY
>STROLLING THE NEVA
>HE'S FUCKING GORGEOUS
>EVGENI ONEGIN

ONEGIN.	**CHORUS.**
AND SO TO THE COUNTRY	HIS SUITS ARE FROM PARIS
I REPAIR,	AHEAD OF THE FASHION
FOR DUTY I DO NOT HOPE TO DARE	HIS FRENCH IS FLAWLESS
FOR BEAUTY,	HE KNOWS HIS BYRON

CHARM,	THE CATCH OF THE CENTURY
AMUSEMENT, FLAIR	STROLLING THE NEVA
	HE'S FUCKING GORGEOUS
	EVGENI ONEGIN
SURPRISE ME!	HIS SUITS ARE FROM PARIS
AMUSE ME,	AHEAD OF THE FASHION
SHAKE ME!	HIS FRENCH IS FLAWLESS
I DARE YOU TRY,	HE KNOWS HIS BYRON
	THE CATCH OF THE CENT'RY
TRY TO WAKE ME!	STROLLING THE NEVA
	HE'S FUCKING GORGEOUS
	EVGENI ONEGIN

I WILL TAKE CARE OF MYSELF	
TO MY HEALTH	
A TOAST, A TOAST	A TOAST, A TOAST
WE ARE GHOSTS, WE ARE GHOSTS	WE ARE GHOSTS
WE ARE GHOSTS	
BONNE SOIRÉE, MA CHERIE, JE T'ADORE	
I DON'T CARE, I DON'T CARE, I DON'T CARE!	
ANYMORE.	

Scene Three

[MUSIC NO. 03A "GARDEN TRANSITION / TO THE GARDEN"]

[MUSIC NO. 04 "IN THE GARDEN"]

(The Larin estate covered in fall leaves.)

*(***OLGA**, **TATYANA**, *and* **MADAME LARIN** *are outside.)*

*(***LENSKY** *and* **ONEGIN** *enter.)*

LENSKY.

MESDAMES! I WANT YOU TO MEET SOMEONE.
MAY I INTRODUCE EVGENI ONEGIN, OUR NEW
  NEIGHBOUR.

ONEGIN.

I'M VERY HONOURED.

*(***ONEGIN** *and* **TATYANA** *have a moment.)*

MADAME LARIN.

HELLO. WE'RE DELIGHTED TO MEET YOU!
THESE ARE MY DAUGHTERS.

ONEGIN.

THE PLEASURE IS MINE.

MADAME LARIN.

COME ALONG INSIDE...
OR PERHAPS YOU'D PREFER TO STAY OUT HERE?
AS OUR NEW NEIGHBOUR – PLEASE, NO NEED TO BE
  FORMAL.

LENSKY.

THIS GARDEN IS ONE OF MY FAVOURITE PLACES.

MADAME LARIN & ONEGIN.

IT IS LOVELY.

MADAME LARIN.

I HAVE TO TEND TO...SOMETHING.

(To the girls.)

ENTERTAIN OUR GUESTS.
I'LL BE BACK RIGHT AWAY.

*(She leaves, indicating to **TATYANA** not to be shy.)*

[MUSIC NO. 05 "TWO SISTERS"]

*(**LENSKY** and **ONEGIN** converse together. **TATYANA** and **OLGA** in their own thoughts:)*

ONEGIN.

WHICH ONE IS TATYANA?

LENSKY.

THE SHY ONE. THE OLDER ONE.

ONEGIN.

AND YOU LOVE THIS OLGA?

LENSKY.

YES. WHY ARE YOU ASKING?

ONEGIN.

I THOUGHT A POET LIKE YOU WOULD'VE CHOSEN THE OTHER.

LENSKY.

WELL MY FRIEND, TWO BEAUTIFUL SISTERS...

TWO SISTERS
POETRY AND PROSE
A LILY AND A ROSE
THE SEA, THE SKY
LIKE YOU AND I

TWO SISTERS
ICE AND FLAME
TWO LOVELY NAMES
TWO LEAVES UPON A TREE
LIKE YOU AND ME

ONEGIN.

OH YES THE STUPID SUN AND THE GLOOMY MOON.

OLGA.

THERE HE IS, MY LENSKY AND THIS ONEGIN
THE NEIGHBOURS WILL HAVE SOMETHING TO SAY ABOUT THAT!
ONEGIN AT OUR HOUSE THEY WILL WHISPER

THEY WILL JOKE THEY WILL TALK AND TALK AND TALK
    AND TALK
MY SISTER, MY SISTER

LENSKY.

TWO SISTERS	**OLGA.**
POETRY AND PROSE	LENSKY
A LILY AND A ROSE	
THE SEA, THE SKY	MY LENSKY
LIKE YOU AND I	
TWO SISTERS ICE AND FLAME	ONE DAY YOU WILL
TWO LOVELY NAMES	PROPOSE TO ME
TWO LEAVES UPON A TREE	I WILL SAY MAYBE...
LIKE YOU AND ME	

ONEGIN.

OH YES THE STUPID SUN AND THE GLOOMY MOON
ON THE HORIZON SING A LONELY TUNE

TATYANA.

HE IS HERE
HE IS HERE
I FEEL IT WAKE ME
THE TURNING WORLD
THE TURNING WORLD
CONSPIRES TO BREAK ME
OPEN
NOW I UNDERSTAND
THE FEELINGS FROM MY BOOKS
HE HAS PIERCED ME WITH A SINGLE LOOK
HE HAS PIERCED ME WITH A SINGLE LOOK

OLGA.	**TATYANA.**	**LENSKY.**	**ONEGIN.**
THERE YOU ARE MY LENSKY	HE IS HERE	TWO SISTERS	STUPID SUN
AND THIS ONEGIN		POETRY AND PROSE	

THE NEIGHBOURS WILL HAVE SOMETHING TO SAY ABOUT THAT	I FEEL IT WAKE ME	A LILY AND A ROSE THE SEA, THE SKY	GLOOMY MOON
		LIKE YOU AND I	
THEY WILL TALK AND TALK AND TALK	THE TURNING WORLD	TWO SISTERS	HORIZON
THEY WILL WHISPER		ICE AND FLAME	
THEY WILL JOKE ABOUT MY SISTER	CONSPIRES TO BREAK ME	TWO LOVELY NAMES TWO LEAVES UPON A TREE LIKE YOU AND ME	LONELY TUNE
	OPEN		OH YES THE STUPID SUN AND THE GLOOMY MOON
MY SISTER			
MY SISTER	OPEN OPEN	TWO SISTERS	ON THE HORIZON SING A LONELY TUNE.

ONEGIN.

MY FRIEND YOU ARE A FOUNTAIN, A DRAMA!
IF I WERE YOU I WOULD HAVE CHOSEN...

OLGA.	**LENSKY.**	**TATYANA.**	**ONEGIN.**
OH, OH MY LENSKY	OLGA!	HE IS HERE	TATYANA!
		HE IS HERE HE IS HERE	

[MUSIC NO. 06 "CAN YOU SEE?"]

(TATYANA and ONEGIN go for a walk, leaving LENSKY and OLGA.)

LENSKY.

CAN YOU SEE HOW HAPPY I AM TO SEE YOU?

OLGA.

VLADIMIR,

WE SAW EACH OTHER YESTERDAY

LENSKY.

OLGA, AN ENTIRE DAY!

DO YOU KNOW HOW LONG THAT IS?

ETERNITY. ETERNITY!

OLGA.

ETERNITY!

YOU KNOW I HATE THAT WORD.

LENSKY.

YES I KNOW

AND YOU KNOW HOW I FEEL

MA PETITE OISEAU.

(OLGA and LENSKY run off.)

(ONEGIN looks nonchalantly at TATYANA, who is standing shyly.)

TATYANA.

SO...YOU'VE JUST MOVED HERE?

ONEGIN.

I AM HERE AT MY UNCLE'S ESTATE

I INHERITED THE PLACE.

TATYANA.

WHAT ABOUT YOUR PARENTS?

ONEGIN.

I BURIED THEM. I BURIED THEM.

YOU DON'T CARE. I DON'T CARE. I DON'T CARE.

I AM HERE AT MY UNCLE'S ESTATE

I INHERITED THE PLACE.

HE WAS A MAN OF THE HIGHEST PRINCIPLES

HE HAD TIME FOR EVERYONE.

WHEN FINALLY HE PASSED ON
THERE WAS NOTHING BUT RESPECT FOR HIM.
BUT CAN I TELL YOU SOMETHING AWFUL?
WHAT A BORE IT WAS, MY GOD
WHAT A CHORE IT WAS, MY GOD
SITTING BY HIS SICKBED
ALWAYS WANTING TO LEAVE.
TELL ME, ISN'T IT TEDIOUS HERE IN THE BARREN
    COUNTRY?
WHAT DO YOU DO FOR FUN?

TATYANA.

NOVELS. I READ NOVELS.

ONEGIN.

I LIKE TO READ AS WELL
BUT YOU CAN'T STAY INSIDE ALL THE TIME.
THE BIRDS HAVE FLOWN ON
HEADED DOWN TO WARMER CLIMES
DO YOU WISH YOU COULD TRAVEL THE WAY THEY DO?
HEAD FOR WARMTH WHEN THE WINTER'S COLD COMES
    THROUGH

TATYANA.

THE BIRDS HAVE FLOWN ON

ONEGIN.

I WON'T BE HERE FOR LONG.

TATYANA & ONEGIN.

DO YOU WISH YOU COULD TRAVEL THE WAY THEY DO?

ONEGIN.

AND YOU? WHAT DO YOU DREAM?

TATYANA.

I DREAM OF A GARDEN
AN OLD HOUSE FULL OF BOOKS.
MY BELOVED...

ONEGIN.

YOUR BELOVED?

TATYANA & ONEGIN.

A DREAM OF A GARDEN

AN OLD HOUSE FULL OF BOOKS

ONEGIN.

> I USED TO DREAM
> BUT THAT WAS LONG AGO.

>> *(They continue their stroll.)*

>> *(**OLGA** and **LENSKY** return.)*

[MUSIC NO. 07 "A PROPOSAL"]

LENSKY.

> OH OLGA, MY DEAR BELOVED DARLING
> MY LONG BELOVED COUNTRY GIRL
> I DELIGHT IN WATCHING AS A STARLING
> I DELIGHT IN HOLDING AS A PEARL
> I LOVE YOU WITH MY WHOLE HEART BEATING
> I COUNT THE HOURS BEFORE EACH MEETING

OLGA.

> VLADIMIR TOGETHER WE WERE CHILDREN
> AT PLAYTIME YOU WERE ALWAYS THERE
> YOU WROTE ME FOOLISH LETTERS BY THE BILLION
> THEN YOU'D TURN AROUND AND PULL MY HAIR
> FOR ME YOU MADE A PEN OUT OF A FEATHER

LENSKY & OLGA.

> TO WRITE A WORLD WHERE WE COULD BE TOGETHER

LENSKY.

> YOU MADE A POET OF ME NOW TAKE PITY

LENSKY & OLGA.

> RELEASE YOUR HEART AND ALL ITS SECRET PARTS

LENSKY.

> PLEASE RECIPROCATE THIS FOOL'S SIMPLICITY
> I LIVE FOR YOU ALONE

LENSKY & OLGA.

> YOU ARE MY OWN
> ALL THAT I CAN OFFER YOU IS WALKS ALONG THE RIVER
> AND CHILDREN ON THE GARDEN LAWN
> I WILL POUR YOU SWEET BLACK TEA
> TO YOU I DEVOTE THE DAWN
> I PROMISE ALL MY FAMILY HAS
> I PROMISE EV'RY MORNING NEW

LENSKY.

> OLGA, I LOVE YOU ETERNALLY
> AND NOTHING WILL KEEP MY LOVE FROM YOU.

OLGA.	**LENSKY.**
VLADIMIR	THIS FRANTIC HEART WAS MADE FOR ADORATION
RELEASE YOUR HEART	RELEASE YOUR HEART
AND ALL ITS SECRET PARTS	AND ALL ITS SECRET PARTS
VLADIMIR	TO LIVE TO DREAM
	TO MAKE THIS PROCLAMATION
	FOR YOU ALONE I LIVE
	FOR YOU ALONE I WRITE
	PLEDGE YOUR HAND TO ME
	THIS NIGHT

OLGA.

> SWEET VLADIMIR,
> WE GREW UP TOGETHER
> HOW I REMEMBER – IT'S FATED.

LENSKY & OLGA.

> FATED.

OLGA.

> I PLEDGE MY HEART TO YOU.

> *(They embrace.)*

> ### [MUSIC NO. 08 "AH, THERE YOU ARE"]

> *(**MADAME LARIN** comes out into the evening dusk and sees them.)*

MADAME LARIN.

> AH, THERE YOU ARE!
> WHERE'S TANYA?

OLGA.

> STROLLING BY THE STREAM.
> WITH ONEGIN.

MADAME LARIN.

IT'S TIME TO SHARE DINNER WITH OUR GUESTS.

LENSKY & OLGA.

WE'RE COMING, MOTHER.

(They joyously go in.)

ONEGIN.

WHEN MY UNCLE NEARED HIS FINAL BREATH
HE LOOKED ME IN THE EYE AND SAID:
"WHEN WILL THE DEVIL COME FOR YOU?"

TATYANA.

"WHEN WILL THE DEVIL COME FOR YOU?"

ONEGIN.

WHAT IS YOUR NAME AGAIN? TATYANA?

TATYANA.

TATYANA LARIN

ONEGIN.	**TATYANA.**
TATYANA LARIN	EVGENI ONEGIN

ONEGIN.

I HAVE SOME BOOKS THAT PERHAPS YOU HAVEN'T READ
I'LL HAVE MY MAN, GUILLOT, BRING THEM OVER

TATYANA.

THAT IS VERY KIND OF YOU

ONEGIN.

OR PERHAPS I COULD BRING THEM MYSELF?

*(**TATYANA** nods.)*

ONEGIN.	**TATYANA.**
TATYANA LARIN	EVGENI ONEGIN

*(**ONEGIN** leaves.)*

TATYANA.

EVGENI ONEGIN.

(She looks around.)

Scene Four

[MUSIC NO. 09 "LET ME DIE"]

*(Tatyana's room. **TATYANA**, lost in thought, getting undressed, then in her nightgown.)*

TATYANA.

OH DEAR FATHER UP IN HEAVEN...
LOOK OUTSIDE THE WINDOW –

Darkness.

I HAVE READ THESE BOOKS
THROUGH THEM I SEE THE WORLD
BUT WHO SEES ME?
WHO KNOWS ME?
AM I ALIVE?

LET ME DIE, LET ME DIE
AS WE ALL MUST DIE
LET ME DIE, LET ME DIE
AS WE ALL MUST DIE
BUT FIRST LA PETITE MORT.
I CALL UPON YOU HOPE
AN ECSTASY THAT I HAVE YET TO KNOW.

BUT OH I HAVE READ BOOKS
THE BOOKS THAT I HAVE READ
PREPARED ME FOR THE LITTLE DEATH
I HAVE ONLY READ BUT NOW I FEEL
EVGENI
I AM DESIRE
LET ME DIE, LET ME DIE AFIRE
I'VE HAD A GLIMPSE, I SEE HIM, ONEGIN
I SEE HIM, I SEE HIM, ONEGIN.

"DEAR EVGENI ONEGIN
I AM WRITING FROM MY HEART."
THEN WHAT?
WHY USE INK WHEN I COULD USE MY VOICE?
WHY WRITE IT HERE WHEN I COULD BREATHE IT SOFTLY
    IN HIS DARLING EAR?

EVGENI ONEGIN...

NO, TANYA, NO.
RETAIN SOME MEASURE OF CONTROL
TANYA, NO.
CONTAIN YOURSELF

LET A LETTER LET SOME ELOQUENCE SHINE THROUGH
IT'S YOU, IT'S YOU, IT'S YOU.

> *(She writes.)*

"EVGENI,
I KNOW YOU ARE SOCIETY
AND HAD YOU NEVER COME TO ME
TO OUR BACKWATER HOME
PERHAPS, MY DEAR
ANOTHER WOULD HAVE CAUGHT MY EAR
ANOTHER MAN WOULD HOLD ME NEAR
BUT NOW I AM UNDONE,
I AM UNDONE
THERE WILL BE NO OTHER MAN, YOU ARE MY ONE
I KNEW THAT YOU WOULD COME."

"ONEGIN,
AS SOON AS YOU WALKED IN MY BELL BEGAN TO RING
THE BRILLIANT SONG WAS CLEAR
THE WORLD DRIFTED
THEN IT STRAIGHTENED OUT AGAIN
BUT BRIGHTER LESS CONTAINED
HE'S HERE,
HE'S HERE
THERE WILL BE NO OTHER MAN
YOU ARE MY ONE
I KNEW THAT YOU WOULD COME!"

> *(She writes. And then:)*

AM I A FOOL?
I BETRAY MYSELF
BUT THIS WILL DESTROY ME IF I KEEP IT CLOSE
I MUST KNOW, I MUST KNOW
I BARE MYSELF

I MUST SHOW, I MUST SHOW YOU ALL I AM, THE BLOOD,
    THE BONE
I IMPLORE YOU,
I IMPLORE YOU
LET ME DIE, LET ME DIE
AS WE ALL MUST DIE
LET ME DIE, LET ME DIE
AS WE ALL MUST DIE...
OH GOD, I AM A FOOL!
AND IF TRULY FACED WITH YOU
WHAT WOULD I DO?
ARE YOU A BEAST,
A SEDUCER
OR WORSE, A TEASE?
A MAN WHO PLAYS AT LOVE?
A MAN WHO PLAYS AT LOVE.

    (She is now singing with a mic on a stand.)

I DON'T CARE
I'M SENDING THIS
I BELIEVE MYSELF
I BELIEVE MY BELL
I WILL STAY THIS COURSE
UNDO MY CORSET'S STAYS
LAY MY HEART OUT AS IT SURELY LAYS
AT YOUR MARVELOUSLY BOOTED FEET
OH GOD
DO WHAT YOU WILL,
DO WHAT YOU WILL,
DO WHAT YOU WILL
WITH ME.

I WILL DIE, I WILL DIE
AS WE ALL MUST DIE.
LET ME DIE, LET ME DIE
AS WE ALL MUST DIE.
BUT FIRST THE LIGHT
BUT FIRST THE SUN
FIRST MY HEART'S TRUE CRY

I LIVE! I LIVE! I LIVE!
BEFORE I DIE.

[MUSIC NO. 10 "GOOD MORNING, SISTER DEAR"]

(Morning. **OLGA** *enters sleepily.)*

GOOD MORNING, SISTER DEAR.

OLGA.

YOU'RE AWAKE ALREADY?

TATYANA.

PLEASE. I NEED YOUR HELP.
WILL YOU SEND THIS TO EVGENI?

OLGA.

ONEGIN? WHAT DOES IT SAY?

TATYANA.

OLGA. OLGA.

OLGA.

SUCH PASSION
SO ROMANTIC.
I'LL SEND IT. TANYA. I'LL SEND IT.

(She sends the letter through the audience to **ONEGIN.***)*

[MUSIC NO. 10A "LETTER MUSIC"]

Scene Five

[MUSIC NO. 11 "LITTLE KISSES"]

(Another part of the Larin estate, the women are drinking tea.)

*(In another place, **ONEGIN** receives Tatyana's letter.)*

OLGA, MADAME LARIN & TATYANA.

ALL OF US WHO GATHER HERE
WE GATHER HERE TO GOSSIP HERE
ALL THE GIRLS ARE PRAYING THAT
GOD BRINGS TO US

WHAT OUR HEART DESIRES
IS A YOUNG MAN, LET HIM BE HANDSOME
WHAT OUR HEART DESIRES
IS TO CATCH HIM AND COVER HIM
WITH WILD BERRIES, NEW CHERRIES
WILD BERRIES, NEW CHERRIES, RED CURRANTS TOO

ALL OF YOU LISTENING TO OUR SWEET GIRLISH SONG
DO YOU KNOW A YOUNG MAN
WHO MIGHT COME ALONG?
TO TAKE US FROM OUR CHORES
TAKE US FROM OUR CHORES
COVER HIM LIKE THIS
WITH OUR LITTLE KISSES
WILD BERRIES, NEW CHERRIES, RED CURRANTS TOO

WE HAVEN'T MUCH TIME
DEAR FATHER UP IN HEAVEN
WE HAVEN'T MUCH TIME
WE DON'T HAVE MUCH TIME.

*(**TATYANA** sees **ONEGIN** arriving.)*

[MUSIC NO. 12 "HE'S HERE"]

TATYANA.

EVGENI. HE'S HERE.
DEAR GOD! DEAR GOD, WHAT DID HE THINK?

WHAT WILL HE SAY?
WHY DID I WRITE HIM?

OLGA.

MOTHER. I HAVE TO SHOW YOU...SOMETHING.

MADAME LARIN.

WHAT IS IT? OH. OOH.

(They move off.)

[MUSIC NO. 13 "ONEGIN'S REFUSAL"]

(ONEGIN *and* **TATYANA** *alone.)*

(He has brought a few books that she hasn't read and gives them to her. She is quietly delighted by the gift.)

ONEGIN.

TATYANA.
I HAVE READ YOUR LETTER
YOU HAVE A TRUSTING HEART.
A NAÏVE HEART.

YOUR HONESTY TOUCHED ME
SINCERELY
YOU HAVE STIRRED FEELINGS LONG ASLEEP
THIS IS THE TRUTH.
YOU HAVE BEEN HONEST WITH ME.
I WILL BE HONEST WITH YOU.

TATYANA.

PLEASE, PLEASE...

ONEGIN. Tatyana. Wait. I am not finished.

IF I WANTED TO LIVE WITHIN A FAM'LY
AS HUSBAND AND FATHER,
THEN YOU ARE WHOM I WOULD CHOOSE
FOR BRIDE AND WIFE AND MOTHER.

I AM NOT MADE FOR THIS,
I AM NOT MADE FOR THIS.
MARRIAGE WOULD BE AGONY, AGONY FOR US.
NO MATTER HOW MUCH I LOVED YOU,
MARRIAGE WOULD KILL ANY PASSION.

DREAMS CANNOT BE RESUMED, CANNOT BE REGAINED
    AFTER WAKING
I CANNOT BE RECIPROCATING.

*(He reaches into his pocket, pulls out several
letters, rifles through them until he finds hers
and holds it out to her.)*

HERE, TAKE BACK YOUR LETTER.
BUT BE CAREFUL WITH YOUR TRUSTING HEART.
YOUR INNOCENT HEART.

ONEGIN.   **TATYANA.**

IF I WANTED TO LIVE   NO.
    WITHIN A FAMILY
AS HUSBAND AND FATHER,
THEN YOU ARE WHOM I   NO.
    WOULD CHOOSE
FOR BRIDE AND WIFE AND
    MOTHER.

ONEGIN & TATYANA.

I AM NOT MADE FOR THIS

ONEGIN.

I AM NOT MADE FOR THIS

TATYANA.
NOT EVERYONE WILL UNDERSTAND YOU
AS I DO.

*(***ONEGIN*** exits.)*

MADAME LARIN & OLGA.

COVER HIM LIKE THIS
WITH OUR LITTLE KISSES **TATYANA.**
WILD BERRIES, NEW   DIE.
    CHERRIES,
RED CURRANTS TOO.   LET ME DIE.

*(***TATYANA*** alone at center.)*

Scene Six

[MUSIC NO. 14 "IT'S RUSSIA, IT'S WINTER"]

(Months go by. Montage. **LENSKY** *and* **OLGA** *walk along the river.* **A MAN** *and* **ANOTHER MAN** *go hunting.* **TATYANA** *watches it all swirl around her. Snow. Until:)*

(In the ballroom of the Larin estate.)

OLGA. Do you know what today is?

TATYANA. January 25?

OLGA. And what does that mean?

TATYANA. *(Shyly.)* It's my name day.

OLGA. Louder!

MADAME LARIN. It's Tatyana's name day! My eldest, such a grown-up woman. Welcome everyone, to our humble home.

(The women perform a welcome dance.)

A MAN.
HOW LONG HAS IT BEEN?

ANOTHER MAN.
I'D SAY WEEKS AT LEAST.
OR MAYBE IT'S MONTHS.

A MAN.
THE WINTERTIME IS LONG

A MAN & ANOTHER MAN.
A MARVELLOUS DANCE
IS JUST WHAT WE NEED.
IT'S RUSSIA, IT'S WINTER
IT'S A LONG TIME AGO.

*(***ONEGIN** *arrives. He and* **TATYANA** *are forced to acknowledge each other awkwardly and then begin to dance together, trying not to make a big deal of it.)*

(A couple of male **GOSSIPS** *chitter-chatter:)*

A MAN.

HAVE YOU SEEN? DID YOU HEAR?

ANOTHER MAN.

IT'S ABOUT TIME. SHE'S GETTING ON.

A MAN.

BUT WITH HIM? BUT WITH HIM?

ANOTHER MAN.

I KNOW!

A MAN.

GOOD LOOKING THOUGH...

ANOTHER MAN.

BUT HE'S NOT TO BE TRUSTED.

A MAN & ANOTHER MAN.

NOT TO BE TRUSTED.

A MAN.

DREADFUL, A ROGUE

ANOTHER MAN.

HE'S JUST PLAIN RUDE.

A MAN.

I HEAR HE KEEPS A GIRL IN MOSCOW

A MAN & ANOTHER MAN.

KEEPS A GIRL IN MOSCOW!

ONEGIN.	**ALL.**
GOSSIPS, THE GOSSIPS	HOW LONG HAS IT BEEN?
SO BORING, THE GOSSIPS!	I'D SAY WEEKS AT LEAST.

*(***LENSKY** *and* **OLGA** *dance by.)*

WHY DID I COME?	OR MAYBE IT'S MONTHS.
LENSKY TWISTED MY ARM	THE WINTERTIME IS LONG.
IT'S HIS FAULT FOR	
DRAGGING ME HERE.	

ONEGIN.

FINE THEN, I'LL FLIRT WITH HIS OLGA.

HIS OLGA.

EVENING, MY DEAR.

MAY I HAVE THE PLEASURE?

LENSKY.

HER DANCE CARD IS FULL.

ONEGIN.

IS IT?

LENSKY. AT EASE, COMRADE.

COME DANCE!
OH OLGA, COME AND DANCE
IT IS A PARTY WITH ME IT IS A PARTY
COME AND DANCE.

OLGA.

MONSIEUR
I'M JUST A COUNTRY GIRL
I BARELY KNOW THE STEPS
YOU'LL HAVE TO SHOW ME

ONEGIN.

OH OLGA, OH OLGA, OH OLGA
COME AND DANCE!
OH OLGA COME AND DANCE
IT IS A PARTY
WITH ME IT IS A PARTY
COME AND DANCE
COME AND DANCE

OLGA

OLGA.

MONSIEUR

DANCE

WITH YOU
MONSIEUR
I'M JUST A COUNTRY GIRL
I BARELY KNOW THE WORLD
YOU'LL HAVE TO SHOW ME
ONEGIN, ONEGIN, ONEGIN
I'LL DANCE

ONEGIN.	**OLGA.**	**CHORUS.**
OH OLGA YES	OH YES	OH DEAR FATHER UP IN HEAVEN
YOU'LL COME AND DANCE	I'LL COME AND DANCE	
IT IS A PARTY	IT IS A PARTY	RELEASE US FROM BOREDOM

WITH ME IT IS A PARTY	WITH YOU IT IS A PARTY	RELEASE US
OH YOU CAN DANCE	I WILL DANCE	BOREDOM
	MONSIEUR	DEAR FATHER, UP IN HEAVEN
YOU'RE JUST A COUNTRY GIRL	I'M JUST A COUNTRY GIRL	
		DEAR FATHER
YOU BARELY KNOW THE WORLD	I BARELY KNOW THE WORLD	
		DEAR FATHER
	YOU'LL HAVE TO SHOW ME!	
OH OLGA!		
	ONEGIN!	
OH OLGA!		
COME AND DANCE	I WILL	
COME AND DANCE!	DANCE!	OH DEAR FATHER UP IN HEAVEN LET THIS DANCE BE GOOD!

ALL.

LUBOV!

(All drink.)

[MUSIC NO. 15 "ONEGIN AND OLGA DANCE"]

*(A sexy dance. **ONEGIN** with **OLGA**.)*

(The dance ends in shocked silence.)

*(**ONEGIN** goes and nonchalantly pours a couple drinks.)*

(**OLGA** *is pulled away by* **TATYANA** *and* **MADAME LARIN**.)

[MUSIC NO. 16 "CALM DOWN"]

(**LENSKY** *goes after* **ONEGIN**.)

LENSKY.

WHAT ARE YOU DOING?

WHY SO CRUEL?

WHAT HAVE I DONE?

ONEGIN.

IT WAS JUST ONE DANCE, JUST ONE DANCE

I TOLD YOU I DIDN'T WANT TO COME

LET IT BE, A LITTLE BIT OF FUN

LENSKY.

MY FEELINGS HAVE MEANINGS!

(*To* **OLGA**.) WILL YOU DANCE THE COTILLION WITH ME?

ONEGIN.

NO, WITH ME. YOU PROMISED ME, DIDN'T YOU?

OLGA.

AND I MUST KEEP MY PROMISE.

STOP BEING SO JEALOUS.

LENSKY.

OLGA.

[MUSIC NO. 17 "THE QUEEN OF TONIGHT"]

WOMEN.

MONSIEUR TRIQUET, MONSIEUR TRIQUET!

TATYANA.

OH NO.

(**TRIQUET** *is making an entrance.*)

ONEGIN.

WHO IS THAT?

MADAME LARIN.

A FRENCHMAN, HE STAYS AT THE KHARLIKOV'S.

A CHANTEUR! HE PERFORMS AT ALL THE PARTIES.

WOMEN.

MONSIEUR TRIQUET, MONSIEUR TRIQUET,

PLEASE SING US A NEW COMPOSITION!

TRIQUET.

> BONJOUR MES AMIS.
> YES, TONIGHT A NEW VERSE.

WOMEN.

> HE SAYS IT'S NEW BUT THEY'RE ALL THE SAME
> HE JUST PUTS IN A DIFF'RENT NAME

TRIQUET.

> WHERE IS MADEMOISELLE?

WOMEN.

> HERE SHE IS! HERE SHE IS!

> (**TATYANA** *is pushed forward.*)

TRIQUET.

> AHA! VOILÀ! THE QUEEN OF TONIGHT.
> MESDAMES, I WILL BEGIN.
> MESSIEURS, GIVE ME SOME ROOM
> TO PAY TRIBUTE TO THE QUEEN.
> LET US ALL PAY HONOUR
> TO THE CHARM AND BEAUTY
> OF THE ONE WHOSE NAME DAY WE NOW CELEBRATE.
> SHE IS SWEET AND KIND
> SPREADS HER GLORY ALL AROUND.
> WHAT A PLEASURE, WHAT A JOY
> SHINE YOUR LOVE UPON US ALL
> FOREVER, BEAUTIFUL TATYANA!
> TATYANA!

CHORUS.

> BRAVO, BRAVO, MONSIEUR TRIQUET!

> (*Mais, he is not finished.*)

TRIQUET.

> *DEUX, TROIS, QUATRE!*
> MAY THE FATES GIVE FAVOUR
> MAY HER MOUTH KNOW PLEASURE
> THAT IT REMAINS ALWAYS WITH A SMILE.
> SHE IS THE NORTH STAR
> SHOWING US THE WAY
> IN THE DARK OF THE NIGHT
> SHINE YOUR LOVE UPON US ALL

FOREVER, BEAUTIFUL TATYANA!
TATYANA!

	CHORUS.
	ALEXANDRA, ANASTASIA,
TRIQUET.	NATASHA, GALINA,
TATYANA!	DARYA,
	KATERINA, ZLATA, OR
	IRINA, ISABELLA,
	KLEMENTINA, LUDMILA,
	MARGARITA,
TATYANA!	NATALYA, ISOLDE,
TATYANA!	SVETLANA,
TATYANA!	SOFIA, ULYANA,
	TATYANA!
TATYANA!	

CHORUS.

BRAVO, BRAVO, BRAVO, MONSIEUR TRIQUET. BRAVO!

(**TRIQUET** *makes a grand bow.*)

[MUSIC NO. 18 "THE COTILLION"]

TRIQUET. Merci, merci! Ladies and gentlemen, take your places please, the cotillion's about to begin!
S'IL VOUS PLAÎT!

(**TRIQUET** *offers* **TATYANA** *his arm and the dance begins.*)

(**ONEGIN** *and* **OLGA** *dance together for a while.*)

(**LENSKY** *sulks with a bottle of vodka.*)

ONEGIN.

YOU'RE NOT DANCING, LENSKY?

LENSKY.

I'D RATHER JUST WATCH.
YOU ARE THE MOST AGILE DANCER.

ONEGIN.

SOMETHING WRONG?

LENSKY.

WHAT DO YOU THINK?

HAVE YOU NOTICED, EV'RYWHERE WE GO, THERE SEEM
TO BE WOMEN TALKING ABOUT YOU?
WHY IS THAT DO YOU THINK?

(The **GUESTS** *slowly stop dancing as they become aware of the tension.)*

OBVIOUSLY, ONE LARIN GIRL IS NOT ENOUGH FOR YOU.

ONEGIN.

IDIOT POET.

LENSKY.

YES. THAT'S RIGHT.
KEEP GOING. KEEP GOING.

(Everybody stops dancing.)

[MUSIC NO. 19 "IN YOUR HOUSE"]

ONEGIN.

LENSKY.

LENSKY.

ONEGIN! I NO LONGER CALL YOU MY FRIEND!
I DESPISE YOU!

ONEGIN.

LISTEN, LENSKY, YOU'RE WRONG,
YOU'RE WRONG!
NOTHING IS GOING ON.

LENSKY.

THEN WHY DO YOU PRESS OLGA'S HAND?
WHY DO YOU WHISPER TO HER?
SHE GIGGLES LIKE A YOUNG GIRL
WHAT DID YOU SAY? WHAT DID YOU DO?

ONEGIN.

THIS IS RIDICULOUS
DON'T SPOIL THE PARTY.
LET'S GO SOMEWHERE AND TALK.

LENSKY.

WHAT DO I CARE?
YOU WASTE YOUR LIFE WITH THESE FUCKING GAMES!
YOU'RE AN INSULT.
GIVE ME SATISFACTION.

OLGA.

VLADIMIR.

MADAME LARIN.

DEAR GOD! IN OUR HOUSE! IN OUR HOUSE.

LENSKY.

IN YOUR HOUSE, IN YOUR HOUSE, IN YOUR HOUSE
AS IN A HONEYED DREAM
MY CHILDHOOD YEARS FLOWED SWEETLY BY!
IN YOUR HOUSE, IN YOUR HOUSE, IN YOUR HOUSE
WHERE I FIRST FOUND

THE JOY OF LOVE THAT COULD BE MINE
BUT IN YOUR HOUSE TONIGHT
I HAVE LEARNED THE TRUTH OF LIFE!

ONEGIN.

I WAS FOOLING AROUND.
IMPULSIVE, AT A PARTY
MY FRIEND, THIS IS NOT THE WAY.

TATYANA.

I CANNOT UNDERSTAND EVGENI
WHAT WAS HE THINKING?

CHORUS.

THE YOUNG MEN HAVE BEEN DRINKING

LENSKY.

IN YOUR HOUSE, IN YOUR HOUSE, IN YOUR HOUSE
TONIGHT
"HONOUR" IS A GHOST!
"FRIEND" AN EMPTY WORD
IN YOUR HOUSE TONIGHT! THIS IS WHAT I HEARD:
A LIE! A LIE! A LIE!

CHORUS.

A NIGHT LIKE THIS, A PARTY
THIS MAY END VERY BADLY IN A DUEL.

ONEGIN.

FOOL! DON'T MAKE ME RAISE MY VOICE

CHORUS.

LENSKY HAS NO CHOICE.

OLGA.

SWEET VLADIMIR, WE GREW UP TOGETHER.

LENSKY.

IN YOUR HOUSE, IN YOUR HOUSE, IN YOUR HOUSE
A YOUNG GIRL
MAY BE BEAUTIFUL AS A MOUNTAIN LAKE
SWEET AND LOVELY AS THE MORNING DEW,
BUT IN HER HEART, HER HEART
HER HEART...

LUBOV!

> (**LENSKY** *grabs a drink, downs it.*)
>
> *(Silence.)*

OLGA.

COME DANCE!
VLADIMIR, COME AND DANCE, IT IS A PARTY
IT IS JUST A PARTY COME AND DANCE!

CHORUS.

YOUNG MEN
SUCH FOOLS
WHY DO THEY QUARREL?
YOUNG MEN
CAN'T KEEP THEMSELVES
IN CHECK!

CHORUS.	**LENSKY.**
YOUNG MEN	THE THING THAT I WAS SURE OF
SUCH FOOLS	WAS AS TRAGIC MISTAKE
WHY DO THEY QUARREL?	MY DREAM HAS VANISHED
YOUNG MEN	BUT I'M GLAD
CAN'T KEEP THEMSELVES	I'M AWAKE.
IN CHECK!	

CHORUS.	**LENSKY.**	**ONEGIN.**
YOUNG MEN	THE THING THAT I WAS SURE OF	WE ARE
SUCH FOOLS	WAS A TRAGIC MISTAKE	GHOSTS

CHORUS.	LENSKY.	ONEGIN.
WHY DO THEY QUARREL?	MY DREAM HAS VANISHED	UPON GHOSTS
YOUNG MEN CAN'T KEEP THEMSELVES IN CHECK!	BUT I'M GLAD I'M AWAKE.	UPON GHOSTS WE ARE GHOSTS

CHORUS.	LENSKY.	ONEGIN.	TATYANA.
YOUNG MEN	THE THING THAT I WAS SURE OF		EVGENI
SUCH FOOLS	WAS AS TRAGIC MISTAKE	WE ARE	A SEDUCER
WHY DO THEY QUARREL?	MY DREAM HAS VANISHED	GHOSTS	A TEASE
YOUNG MEN	BUT I'M GLAD	UPON GHOSTS	A MAN WHO PLAYS
CAN'T KEEP THEMSELVES IN CHECK!	I'M AWAKE.	UPON GHOSTS WE ARE GHOSTS	AT LOVE

CHORUS.	LENSKY.	ONEGIN.	TATYANA.	OLGA.
YOUNG MEN	THE THING THAT I WAS SURE OF		EVGENI	VLADIMIR
SUCH FOOLS	WAS AS TRAGIC MISTAKE	WE ARE	A SEDUCER	MY HEART, MY DEAR
WHY DO THEY QUARREL?	MY DREAM HAS VANISHED	GHOSTS	A TEASE	VLADIMIR
YOUNG MEN	BUT I'M GLAD	UPON GHOSTS	A MAN WHO PLAYS	YOU FOOLS, CALM DOWN

CAN'T KEEP	I'M AWAKE.	UPON	AT LOVE	CALM
THEMSELVES		GHOSTS		DOWN
IN CHECK!		WE ARE		
		GHOSTS		

LENSKY.

I WILL PUNISH MY FRIENDLESS FORMER FRIEND

ONEGIN.

I SHOULD KNOW BETTER THAN TO FOOL WITH
CHILDREN.

CHORUS.

AN INSULT! LEADS TO A CHALLENGE! LEADS TO A DUEL!

TATYANA.

DOOMED.

CHORUS.

A DUEL?

OLGA & MADAME LARIN.

NO!

CHORUS.

A DUEL!

ONEGIN.

THERE'S NOTHING TO BE DONE –
YOU'VE GONE INSANE.
I AM AT YOUR SERVICE.

CHORUS.

AN INSULT!
LEADS TO A CHALLENGE!
LEADS TO AGREEMENT!

ONEGIN.

I ACCEPT.

LENSKY.

TOMORROW, THEN.
YES, I AM INSANE.
BUT NOT DISHONOURABLE.

ONEGIN.

YOU WANT ME TO KILL YOU NOW?
I'LL KILL YOU!

*(**ONEGIN** hurls himself upon **LENSKY**. The two
men are separated and restrained.)*

WOMEN.   **MEN.**

   QUELLE SCANDAL!   FOOLISH YOUTH!

   AH!   HOLD THEM NOW!

   AH!   NO BLOODSHED IN THE

   AH!   LARIN HOUSE!

OLGA.

   VLADIMIR!

LENSKY.

   TOMORROW. DOWN BY THE RIVER. AT DAWN.

ALL.

   AN INSULT!

   A CHALLENGE!

   AGREEMENT!

   A SHOT!

LENSKY.

   OH OLGA,

   FAREWELL!

      *(**LENSKY** rushes out.)*

      (Intermission.)

ACT TWO

Scene Seven

[MUSIC NO. 20 "GOOD EVENING, BONNE SOIRÉE"]

OLGA, TATYANA & MADAME LARIN.

AH...

LENSKY. Welcome back. We're going to keep going. Hope that's all right with you.

(Audience responds.)

A MAN. Lubov!

(All drink.)

One thing we forgot to mention about this band. They are all in the other place.

ANOTHER MAN. *(Cellist.)* Cholera. *(Drummer.)* A farming accident. *(Pianist.)* Old age.

A MAN. They aren't in heaven exactly. Now they play for us. You can decide where you think that might be. The Ungrateful Dead.

*(The **ENSEMBLE** places candles everywhere through the following.)*

WOMEN.	MEN.
A LOVE SONG WE SING TO YOU	AH
WE HOPE THAT YOU MIGHT HEAR IT	
OH HOW WE LOVE TO DREAM OF LOVE	AH
INVITING PUSHKIN'S SPIRIT.	

LENSKY.

GOOD EVENING. BONNE SOIRÉE.
A PARTY. DELIGHTFUL. DELIGHTED. ENCHANTÉ,
GOOD EVENING. BONNE SOIRÉE.

TATYANA & LENSKY.

> GOOD EVENING. BONNE SOIRÉE.
> A PARTY. DELIGHTFUL. DELIGHTED. ENCHANTÉ,
> GOOD EVENING. BONNE SOIRÉE.

ALL.

> GOOD EVENING. BONNE SOIRÉE.
> A PARTY. DELIGHTFUL. DELIGHTED. ENCHANTÉ,
> GOOD EVENING. BONNE SOIRÉE.

ONEGIN.

> A TOAST, A TOAST TO THAT BLOODSTAINED GHOST,
> THAT VISITS AND TELLS ME EV'RY DAY
> EV'RYWHERE WILL BE THE SAME
> EV'RYWHERE WILL BE THE SAME

ALL.

> GOOD EVENING. BONNE SOIRÉE.
> A PARTY. DELIGHTFUL. DELIGHTED. ENCHANTÉ,
> GOOD EVENING. BONNE SOIRÉE.

LENSKY, ONEGIN & TATYANA.

> A TOAST, A TOAST TO THAT BLOODSTAINED GHOST, THAT
> VISITS AND QUESTIONS ME ANEW!

LENSKY.

> WHEN WILL THE DEVIL COME FOR YOU?

TATYANA.

> WHEN WILL THE DEVIL COME FOR YOU?

ONEGIN.

> WHEN WILL THE DEVIL COME FOR YOU?

Scene Eight

[MUSIC NO. 21 "RULES FOR DUELING"]

(ZARETSKY officiously explains all the rules he's about to screw up:)

ZARETSKY.
RULES FOR DUELING
THE MEN AGREE ON A TIME AND PLACE
ONE MUSTN'T HESITATE
A QUARTER HOUR LATE
INDICATES A FORFEIT

WOMEN.
YOUR FATE

ZARETSKY.
THE SECONDS, MEN OF CLASS, WILL ASK
FOR AN APOLOGY
IF NONE FORTHCOMES
THE DUEL PROCEEDS

WOMEN.
YOUR DESTINY...

ZARETSKY.
THE SECONDS,

WOMEN.
WHO ARE GENTLEMEN OF CLASS!

ZARETSKY.
MEASURE OUT THE SHOOTING DISTANCE
ONE TWO THREE FOUR FIVE SIX SEVEN EIGHT NINE TEN
    TWENTY THIRTY YARDS
THE ADVERSARIES TAKE THEIR POSITIONS
FACING ONE ANOTHER
PISTOLS AT THEIR SIDES
AT MY SIGNAL

(Three claps.)

THE MEN APPROACH AND FIRE!
I AM PRECISE!

WOMEN.
A GENTLEMAN OF CLASS!

ALL.

>UN DEUX TROIS QUATRE CINQ SIX SEPT HUIT NEUF DIX
>>VINGTY TRENTE-TY YARDS

ZARETSKY.

>THE ADVERSARIES TAKE THEIR POSITIONS
>FACING ONE ANOTHER
>PISTOLS AT THEIR SIDES
>AT MY SIGNAL

>>*(Three claps.)*

>THE MEN APPROACH AND FIRE! I AM PRECISE!

ALL.

>A GENTLEMAN OF CLASS!

ZARETSKY.

>THIS DUEL SHALL RUN CORRECTLY
>OR MY NAME IS NOT MONSIEUR ZARETSKY!

[MUSIC NO. 22 "ON THE BANKS"]

>*(On the banks of a wooded stream. Early morning.* **LENSKY,** *lost in thought.* **ZARETSKY** *is pacing.)*

>ON THE BANKS OF THIS WOODED STREAM
>EARLY MORNING
>THE SUN HAS YET TO RISE
>HAVE YOU SEEN YOUR OPPONENT?

LENSKY.

>NOT YET.

ZARETSKY.

>WE WERE HERE ON TIME.
>KEEP AN EYE OUT.
>HE'S ELEVEN MINUTES LATE.

WOMEN.

>A QUARTER HOUR LATE INDICATES
>A FORFEIT.

[MUSIC NO. 23 "OLGA, WILL YOU WEEP?"]

LENSKY.

>TODAY, TODAY
>THE SUN WILL RISE

THE WORLD WILL SEE THE DAWN
BUT WILL I? WILL I?

TODAY, TODAY
THE WORLD WILL WAKE
AND PUT THE COFFEE ON
I WOULD MISS THESE DAYS
I WOULD MISS THEM
IF I WERE GONE.

OH OLGA, WILL YOU WEEP?
OH OLGA, WILL YOU WEEP?
MY ORCHID IN THE COUNTRY
YOU WERE LOVED BY ME.

TODAY, TODAY
THEY'LL STRIP THE SHEETS
WASH THE LAUNDRY THEN
HANG TO DRY, HANG TO DRY
SOMEWHERE TODAY THEY'LL HUNT A DEER
SOMEWHERE TONIGHT THEY'LL FEAST
BUT WILL I?

PERHAPS HIS BULLET WILL FLY WIDE
I WILL WALK BACK TO YOUR SIDE
THE BIRDSONG WILL BE SWEET
PERHAPS HIS BULLET FINDS ITS MARK
MY HEART, MY HEART, MY HEART

LENSKY.	CHORUS.
OH OLGA, WILL YOU WEEP?	OOH
OH OLGA, WILL YOU WEEP?	OOOOH
MY ORCHID IN THE COUNTRY	
YOU WERE LOVED BY ME	
OH OLGA, PLEASE RECALL	AHH
OLGA, PLEASE RECALL	AHH
THOSE NIGHTS ALONG THE RIVER	
WHEN WE BOTH DID FALL	AHH
OLGA WILL YOU WEEP, OLGA WILL YOU WEEP	OOO OOO
WILL YOU WEEP FOR ME?	

(**OLGA** *appears as in a dream and they walk.*)

LENSKY.

OLGA, I LOVE YOU
AND TO YOU ALONE I DEVOTE THE SAD DAWN
I DID NOT SLEEP THIS NIGHT
THE WORLD MAY SEE MY END
A YOUNG POET FORGOTTEN

(**OLGA** *disappears.*)

CHORUS.

LOOK AROUND, LOOK AROUND, LOOK AROUND
DO YOU SEE SOMEONE WORTH DYING FOR?

LENSKY.

TODAY, TODAY
THE SUN WILL RISE
THE WORLD WILL SEE THE DAWN.

(**ONEGIN** *appears.*)

[MUSIC NO. 24 "I'M A LITTLE LATE"]

ONEGIN.

FORGIVE ME.
I'M A LITTLE LATE.

ZARETSKY.

YES.

WOMEN.

A QUARTER HOUR LATE INDICATES A FORFEIT.

ZARETSKY.

I AM ZARETSKY
WHERE IS YOUR SECOND?
WHERE DUELING'S CONCERNED,
I'M PARTICULARLY PARTICULAR
I FOLLOW THE OLD TRADITION!

ONEGIN.

ALL WILL PRAISE YOU
MY SECOND IS MONSIEUR GUILLOT.

ZARETSKY.

YOUR SERVANT?

WOMEN.

THE SECONDS WHO ARE GENTLEMEN OF CLASS.

ONEGIN.

IF YOU FIND THAT UNACCEPTABLE –

ZARETSKY.

ENOUGH! LET THE DUEL BEGIN!

WOMEN.

YOUNG MEN, SUCH FOOLS, WHY DO THEY QUARREL?
YOUNG MEN CAN'T KEEP THEMSELVES IN CHECK.

[MUSIC NO. 25 "MY DEAREST COMRADE"]

(**ONEGIN** and **LENSKY** prepare each other as if they were going out to party together.)

(**TATYANA** and **OLGA** in other places.)

ONEGIN & LENSKY. (Staggered.)

MY DEAREST COMRADE
NOW MY PRESENT RIVAL
MY DEAREST COMRADE NOW MY RIVAL
HOW LONG? HOW LONG?
MY DEAREST COMRADE
NOW MY PRESENT RIVAL
MY DEAREST COMRADE NOW MY RIVAL
HOW LONG? HOW LONG?

ONEGIN.	**LENSKY.**
IS THIS JUSTIFIED?	IS THIS JUSTIFIED REVENGE?
	WHAT HAPPENED TO
MY FRIEND?	MY FRIEND?

ONEGIN & LENSKY.

THIS IS LAUGHABLE HA HA HA HA HA HA HA HA HA HA
THIS IS LAUGHABLE HA HA HA HA HA HA HA HA HA HA
IF I WAS WATCHING THIS IT WOULD MAKE ME LAUGH

(Staggered.)

MY DEAREST COMRADE
NOW MY PRESENT RIVAL
MY DEAREST COMRADE NOW MY RIVAL

HOW LONG? HOW LONG?
MY DEAREST COMRADE
NOW MY PRESENT RIVAL
MY DEAREST COMRADE NOW MY RIVAL
HOW LONG? HOW LONG?

ONEGIN.   **LENSKY.**

IS THIS JUSTIFIED   IS THIS JUSTIFIED?
REVENGE?

WHAT HAPPENED TO

MY FRIEND?   MY FRIEND?

ONEGIN & LENSKY.

THIS IS LAUGHABLE HA HA HA HA HA HA HA HA HA
THIS IS LAUGHABLE HA HA HA HA HA HA HA HA HA
IF I WAS WATCHING THIS
IT WOULD MAKE ME LAUGH

OLGA.

IT WAS JUST ONE DANCE, JUST ONE DANCE
I TAKE IT BACK
MY LENSKY, OH MY LENSKY
YOU ARE ALL I HAVE.

TATYANA.   **OLGA.**

LOOK   HA HA HA AH HA
OUTSIDE THE WINDOW   HA HA HA AH HA
I HAVE READ THESE   HA HA HA AH HA
   BOOKS
BUT THIS IS NOT THE   HA HA HA AH HA
   WORLD
WHO SEES ME?   ALL I
WHO KNOWS ME?   HAVE

		ONEGIN & LENSKY.
OLGA.	**TATYANA.**	*(Staggered.)*
IT WAS JUST ONE DANCE	HA HA	MY DEAREST COMRADE
JUST ONE DANCE	HA AH HA	NOW MY PRESENT RIVAL

I TAKE IT BACK		
MY LENSKY,	HA HA	MY DEAREST COMRADE
OH MY LENSKY	HA AH HA	NOW MY PRESENT RIVAL
IT WAS JUST ONE DANCE	HA HA	MY DEAREST COMRADE
JUST ONE DANCE	HA AH HA	NOW MY PRESENT RIVAL
I TAKE IT BACK		
MY LENSKY,	HA HA	MY DEAREST COMRADE
OH MY LENSKY	HA AH HA	NOW MY PRESENT RIVAL

ONEGIN & LENSKY. *(Staggered.)*
> WILL YOU SAY SOMETHING
> TO HALT THIS VIOLENT GAME
> WE WERE THE SAME

> *(They both have shot glasses filled with vodka.)*

ONEGIN.
> WHAT DO YOU SAY?

LENSKY.
> WHAT DO I SAY?

> *(**LENSKY** sees an image of **OLGA**.)*

> NYET.

ONEGIN & LENSKY.
> NYET.
> NO.

> *(**LENSKY** and **ONEGIN** down the shots.)*

> **[MUSIC NO. 26 "THE DUEL"]**

ALL.
> *AN INSULT!*

A CHALLENGE! AGREEMENT!
A RENDEZVOUS!

> (**ONEGIN** *and* **LENSKY** *get pistols from* **ZARETSKY.**)
>
> (**GUILLOT** *hides behind something.*)
>
> (**ZARETSKY** *gives the signal.*)
>
> (*Back to back. Then paces.*)

WOMEN.

AH AH AH AH

> (**CHORUS** *claps three times.*)

AH

> (*A shot.*)
>
> (**LENSKY** *falls.* **ONEGIN** *goes to him.*)
>
> (**ONEGIN** *drops to one knee.*)
>
> (**LENSKY** *rises and joins the band. The band gives him a glass. They all raise a glass.*)

CHORUS.

WHEN WILL THE DEVIL COME FOR YOU?
WHEN WILL THE DEVIL COME FOR YOU?

LENSKY.

LUBOV!

> (*Drinks.*)

Scene Nine

[MUSIC NO. 27 "GOOD EVENING, BONNE SOIRÉE – REPRISE"]

(**ZARETSKY** *gathers the pistols. The* **WOMEN** *clean up the snow.*)

(**TATYANA** *looks at* **ONEGIN**.)

TATYANA.

YOU DON'T CARE, YOU DON'T CARE, YOU DON'T CARE, YOU DON'T CARE,

YOU DON'T CARE, YOU DON'T CARE, YOU DON'T CARE, YOU DON'T CARE

(**TATYANA** *leaves.* **ONEGIN** *crumples.*)

CHORUS.

AH

(*Six years pass.*)

(*A mansion in Saint Petersburg. Another party.*)

PRINCE GREMIN.

Welcome to Saint Petersburg!

ONEGIN.

I'VE TRAVELLED AND TRAVELLED

THE CHANGING SCENERY

I HOPED IT WOULD, I HOPED IT WOULD, I HOPED IT WOULD CHANGE ME

A TOAST, A TOAST TO THAT BLOODSTAINED GHOST

THAT VISITS AND TELLS ME EVERY DAY

CHORUS.

EV'RYWHERE WILL BE THE SAME,

EV'RYWHERE WILL BE THE SAME,

EV'RYWHERE WILL BE THE SAME

ONEGIN.

SURPRISE ME,

AMUSE ME, SHAKE ME

CHORUS.

    EV'RYWHERE WILL BE THE SAME

ONEGIN.

    I DARE YOU TRY

    TRY TO WAKE ME

CHORUS.

    EV'RYWHERE WILL BE THE SAME

ONEGIN.

    SURPRISE ME, AMUSE ME, SHAKE ME

    I DARE YOU TRY

    TRY TO WAKE ME

ALL.

    A TOAST, A TOAST TO THAT BLOODSTAINED GHOST

ONEGIN.

    THAT HAUNTS ME

    EVERY DAY.

    (A couple of female **GOSSIPS** *chitter-chatter:)*

WOMAN 1.

    WHO IS THAT?

WOMAN 2.

    IS THAT?

WOMAN 1.

    WHO?

WOMAN 2.

    IT'S ONEGIN

WOMAN 1.

    HE'S BACK

WOMAN 2.

    LENSKY SO TRAGIC

WOMAN 1.

    SO SAD

WOMAN 2.

    WHAT HAPPENED TO THE FIANCÉE?

WOMAN 1.

    OLGA LARIN?

    SHE WAS NEVER THE SAME

SHE WEPT,
SHE MENDED
SHE DIDN'T FORGET HER POET
SHE MOVED AWAY

WOMAN 1 & 2.

SHE WEPT,
SHE MENDED
SHE DIDN'T FORGET HER POET
SHE MOVED AWAY

WOMAN 2.

FOUND A SOLDIER IN MOSCOW

CHORUS.

A GOOD SOLDIER IN MOSCOW
GOOD EVENING. BONNE SOIRÉE.
A PARTY. DELIGHTFUL. DELIGHTED. ENCHANTÉ,
GOOD EVENING. BONNE SOIRÉE.

WOMAN 1.

IT'S BEEN WHAT?

WOMAN 2.

SIX YEARS.

WOMAN 1.

SIX YEARS!

WOMAN 2.

GIVE OR TAKE.

WOMAN 1.

HE LOOKS OLDER.

WOMAN 2.

SO DO YOU.

WOMAN 1.

SO DO YOU.

ALL.

SO DO YOU!

OH DEAR FATHER UP IN HEAVEN
RELEASE US FROM BOREDOM
OH DEAR FATHER UP IN HEAVEN
SEND US A GOOD TIME.
OH DEAR FATHER UP IN HEAVEN

LOOK DOWN AT US SMILING
OH DEAR FATHER MAKE IT HAPPEN TONIGHT!

[MUSIC NO. 28 "ÉCOSSAISE"]

(The **GUESTS** *dance an écossaise.)*

[MUSIC NO. 29 "WELCOME MY OLD FRIEND"]

PRINCE GREMIN.

WELCOME MY OLD FRIEND.
THE TOWN IS YOURS.

ONEGIN.

WITH PLEASURE, PRINCE GREMIN.
IT FEELS ODD TO BE BACK.
TELL ME, DO YOU HAPPEN TO KNOW
THE WOMAN...
BY THE FAR WALL?

PRINCE GREMIN.

AH! IT HAS BEEN SOME TIME SINCE YOU WERE LAST IN
SOCIETY.

ONEGIN.

YES. I HAVE BEEN TRAVELLING.

PRINCE GREMIN.

SHALL I INTRODUCE YOU?

ONEGIN.

BUT WHO IS SHE?

*(**PRINCE GREMIN** smiles.)*

[MUSIC NO. 30 "AGE DOESN'T MATTER TO LOVE"]

PRINCE GREMIN.

AGE DOESN'T MATTER TO LOVE
LOVE COMES
TO THE YOUNG
WHO KNOW NOTHING
AND TO THE GREY SOLDIER LOVE COMES
THOUGH HE HAD STEELED HIMSELF FROM EMOTION
ONEGIN

I CAN'T HIDE IT
I LOVE HER!

AS MY LIFE SLIPPED AWAY
SHE APPEARED, SHE APPEARED, SHE APPEARED!
SUNLIGHT ON A STORMY DAY
AND BROUGHT ME A NEW AGE

LOOK AROUND, LOOK AROUND, LOOK AROUND
FOOLISH CHILDREN
BORES, COQUETTES
VAMPS AND FLIRTS
AND GOSSIPS AND LIARS AND DRUNK POSEURS
WEARING THE RIGHT CLOTHES
SAYING THE RIGHT WORDS

LOOK AROUND, LOOK AROUND, LOOK AROUND
SEE HOW SHE SHINES ABOVE THEM
IN THE DARK OF THE NIGHT
SHE IS THE NORTHERN STAR
SHE APPEARED, SHE APPEARED, SHE APPEARED!
SUNLIGHT ON A STORMY DAY
AND BROUGHT ME A NEW AGE.

AGE DOESN'T MATTER TO LOVE
LOVE COMES
TO THE YOUNG
WHO KNOW NOTHING
AND TO THE GREY SOLDIER LOVE COMES
THOUGH HE HAD STEELED HIMSELF FROM EMOTION

ONEGIN,
I CAN'T HIDE IT
I LOVE HER
LIKE I WAS YOUNG
LIKE I KNOW NOTHING.

    (**TATYANA** *appears, the epitome of grace.*)

ALL.

LOOK AROUND, LOOK AROUND, LOOK AROUND
SEE HOW SHE SHINES ABOVE US
IN THE DARK OF THE NIGHT

SHE IS THE NORTHERN STAR
SHE APPEARED, SHE APPEARED, SHE APPEARED!
SUNLIGHT ON A STORMY DAY
AND BROUGHT HIM A NEW AGE.

(**PRINCE GREMIN** *and* **TATYANA** *dance.*)

PRINCE GREMIN.

ANGEL, ALLOW ME TO INTRODUCE
AN OLD FRIEND OF MINE
ONEGIN, TATYANA.

ONEGIN.

TATYANA.

PRINCE GREMIN.

ONEGIN, TATYANA MY WIFE.

(**ONEGIN** *bows.*)

ONEGIN.

SO YOU'VE MARRIED?
I DIDN'T KNOW. HOW LONG?

PRINCE GREMIN.

TWO YEARS AND TWENTY-THREE DAYS.
GIVE OR TAKE.

ALL.

AGE DOESN'T MATTER TO LOVE.

(**PRINCE GREMIN** *gives them some room.*)

[MUSIC NO. 31 "MAY WE GO"]

TATYANA.

I WAS NOT SURE I'D EVER SEE YOU AGAIN.

ONEGIN.

IT HAS BEEN SIX YEARS.

TATYANA.

HOW IS YOUR PLACE IN THE COUNTRY?

ONEGIN.

I HAVE NOT BEEN THERE FOR QUITE AWHILE. YOU MUST
KNOW.

TATYANA.

YES.

ONEGIN.

I'VE BEEN ABROAD.

TATYANA.

HOW LONG HAVE YOU BEEN BACK?

ONEGIN.

ONLY TODAY. ONLY TODAY.

TATYANA. *(To* **PRINCE GREMIN.***)*

MY PRINCE, I AM TIRED. MAY WE GO?

> (**TATYANA** *leaves on* **PRINCE GREMIN***'s arm.*
> **ONEGIN** *watches them go.)*

[MUSIC NO. 32 "TO LIVE IN LOVE"]

CHORUS.

TATYANA!

SEE HOW SHE SHINES ABOVE US!

IF I WANTED TO LIVE, IN LOVE, IN LOVE

THEN YOU ARE WHOM I WOULD CHOOSE...

Scene Ten

[MUSIC NO. 33 "SAINT PETERSBURG"]

(The streets of Saint Petersburg.)

*(**ONEGIN** writes letters. He sends them through the audience to **TATYANA**.)*

*(In another place, **TATYANA** receives them and reads.)*

ONEGIN. *(Writing.)* Our time is precious. I find myself back in Petersburg, the city of my youth, and all I do is drag myself from café to café, dreaming of when I will see you again.

I am interested in nothing else.

Chance first brought us together. Chance has found us again.

CHORUS.
> SAINT PETERSBURG, A YOUNG CITY
> BEAUTY BUILT OUT OF THE WOOD AND MIRE
> IT'S EIGHTEEN TWENTY-FIVE.

> THE CITY SEETHING WITH UNREST
> REVOLUTION MUTTERED UNDER BREATH
> IT'S THAT OR DEATH.

> THE RIVER NEVA SLOWLY LABOURS
> BENEATH GRACEFUL BRIDGES, GARDENS COVER
> THE ONCE BARE ISLES THAT DOT THE RIVER
> ITS ICY SURFACE COLD AND GREY
> SAINT PETERSBURG, ANOTHER DAY.

ONEGIN. *(Writing.)* I can see now the happiness you have found. No! That you have always possessed.

I have learned that this is what is most important. Please forgive me.

I was not able to understand this when we first met.

The die is cast. My fate is with you and no one else.

You are my life.

WOMEN.
> A LOVE SONG I SING TO YOU

CHORUS.

> SAINT PETERSBURG, A DAY GOES BY
> ONEGIN SITS ALONE AT A CAFÉ
> GOES BY A DAY

ONEGIN.

> I BETRAY MYSELF, MY DEAR TATYANA.

WOMEN.

> OH, HOW WE LOVE TO DREAM OF LOVE

CHORUS.

> THE CITY PUSHES FURTHER ON
> ONEGIN SITS AND WRITES

WOMEN.

> A LOVE SONG

CHORUS.

> ANOTHER DAY IS GONE

ONEGIN.

> I CAN'T BELIEVE IT'S TRUE
> JUST SIX YEARS AGO, THIS WAS YOU

WOMEN.

> UNTETHER NOW FROM DAY TO DAY

CHORUS.

> THE RIVER NEVA SLOWLY LABOURS

WOMEN.

> THE ARCHER LETS AN ARROW FLY

CHORUS.

> BENEATH GRACEFUL BRIDGES GARDENS COVER

WOMEN.

> WILL THE ARROW HIT ITS MARK?

CHORUS.

> THE ONCE BARE ISLES THAT DOT THE RIVER

WOMEN.

> ONCE WE MAKE LOVE IS IT HERE TO STAY?

CHORUS.

> SAINT PETERSBURG, ANOTHER DAY.

TATYANA.

> HE IS HERE,
> HE IS HERE

I FEEL IT WAKE ME

THE TURNING WORLD CONSPIRES TO BREAK ME

ONEGIN.

I AM YOURS

TATYANA.

OPEN

ONEGIN.

I AM AWAKE

TATYANA.

OPEN

ONEGIN.

I AM HERE

TATYANA.

HERE

ONEGIN.

I AM HERE

CHORUS.

ONCE WE MAKE LOVE IT IS HERE TO STAY

(Letters fill the sky.)

ONEGIN.

FOREVER

CHORUS.

BUT WHERE IT LANDS

ONEGIN.

BEAUTIFUL

CHORUS.

AND HOW IT ENDS

CHORUS.		**ONEGIN.**
THAT IS HARD TO		TATYANA.
SAY.	**TATYANA.**	
	WHO SEES ME?	
THAT IS HARD TO		TATYANA,
SAY.		
	WHO KNOWS	
	ME?	

SAINT   WHO?   TATYANA,
   PETERSBURG   TATYANA.
SAINT   TATYANA,
   PETERSBURG   TATYANA.

ALL.
   ANOTHER DAY!

Scene Eleven

[MUSIC NO. 34 "THE SIGNAL"]

(**ONEGIN** *with a vision of* **LENSKY** *from the first hunting scene.*)

ONEGIN.

ONE TWO THREE FOUR FIVE SIX AWFUL EMPTY YEARS
LENSKY, WHAT HAVE YOU MISSED?

(**LENSKY** *with* **OLGA.**)

I HATE TO BE ALIVE
BUT THIS FEELING, THIS FEELING
TAKES ME BACK IN TIME.
THIS IS A SIGNAL.

(**LENSKY** *taps his chest three times.*)

IN YOUR NAME VLADIMIR
I WILL NOT WASTE MY LIFE.

(**LENSKY**'s *ghost disappears into the band.*)

[MUSIC NO. 35 "ONCE MORE, ONEGIN"]

TATYANA.

ONCE MORE, ONEGIN
LIKE SOME RESTLESS, RESTLESS GHOST
HIS EYES
AWAKE MY PASSION
I AM A YOUNG GIRL AGAIN,
I AM A YOUNG GIRL AGAIN
WITH DREAMS OF A GARDEN
AN OLD HOUSE FULL OF BOOKS
MY BELOVED

(**ONEGIN** *enters.*)

ONEGIN.

TATYANA.
I SEE YOU.
AT LAST I SEE YOU.

(*Pause.*)

TATYANA.

> ONEGIN, I WAS YOUNGER THEN
> I LOVED YOU BUT FOR WHAT
> YOU KNOW HOW YOU RECEIVED
> A SIMPLE YOUNG GIRL'S LOVE

ONEGIN.

> TATYANA, I WAS YOUNGER THEN
> NOW THE VEIL HAS RISEN
> YOUR CRYING EYES ARE DEAR TO ME
> I BEG TO BE FORGIVEN.

> *(***ONEGIN*** drops to his knees.)*

TATYANA.

> AGAIN, ONEGIN
> YOUR GHOST WILL NOT RELENT
> ENOUGH, GET UP, GET UP!
> DO YOU REMEMBER
> IN THE GARDEN?
> I LISTENED
> WHILE YOU LECTURED ME
> YOU LECTURED ME ON LOVE.

> BUT I WILL GIVE YOU THIS
> IN THAT DREADFUL TIME
> YOU DID NOT TAKE ADVANTAGE
> AS YOU REFUSED MY DESIRE.

> WHY THEN, ONEGIN
> WHY DO YOU PURSUE ME NOW?
> WHY? DO I MERIT SUCH ATTENTION
> COULD IT BE BECAUSE I AM SOCIETY
> WITH BANKS OF MONEY?

ONEGIN.

> PLEASE.

TATYANA. I am not finished.

> I HAVE A HUSBAND WHOM I CHERISH
> A HERO WHO IS LOVED.
> AND NOW, WILL YOU LECTURE ME?
> YOU WHO WERE ONCE SO PROUD
> WHY DO YOU SUPPOSE THAT YOU DESIRE ME NOW?

ONEGIN.

TATYANA, I WAS YOUNGER THEN

TATYANA.

EVGENI, I WAS YOUNGER THEN

ONEGIN.

I BEG TO BE FORGIVEN

TATYANA.

I LOVED YOU AND I LEARNED

ONEGIN.

YOUR CRYING EYES ARE DEAR TO ME

TATYANA.

YOU KNOW HOW YOU RESPONDED
TO THE LOVE OF A YOUNG GIRL

ONEGIN.

WITH DREAMS OF A GARDEN.
AN OLD HOUSE FULL OF BOOKS
MY BELOVED.

ONEGIN & TATYANA.

YOUR BELOVED.

TATYANA.	**ONEGIN.**
ONEGIN, I WAS YOUNGER THEN	TATYANA, I WAS YOUNGER THEN
I LOVED YOU BUT FOR WHAT	NOW THE VEIL HAS RISEN
YOU KNOW HOW YOU RECEIVED	YOUR CRYING EYES ARE DEAR TO ME
A SIMPLE YOUNG GIRL'S LOVE	I BEG TO BE FORGIVEN
ONEGIN, I WAS YOUNGER THEN	TATYANA, I WAS YOUNGER THEN
I LOVED YOU BUT FOR WHAT	NOW THE VEIL HAS RISEN
YOU KNOW HOW YOU RECEIVED	YOUR CRYING EYES ARE DEAR TO ME
A SIMPLE YOUNG GIRL'S LOVE	I BEG TO BE FORGIVEN

ONEGIN.

> I WAS A FOOL!
> I BETRAY MYSELF
> BUT THIS WILL DESTROY ME
> IF I KEEP IT CLOSE
>
> I MUST KNOW, I MUST KNOW
> I BARE MYSELF
> I MUST SHOW, I MUST SHOW YOU ALL I AM
> THE BLOOD, THE BONE
> I IMPLORE YOU,
> I IMPLORE YOU
> I WILL DIE, I WILL DIE AS WE ALL MUST DIE
> LET ME DIE,
> LET ME DIE
> AS WE ALL MUST DIE
> TATYANA,
>
> CAN WE GO BACK IN TIME?
> BEFORE IT ALL WENT WRONG
> I KNOW THAT I HAVE CHANGED.
> I WAS A MAN WHO PLAYED AT LIFE
> A MAN WHO PLAYED AT LIFE.

TATYANA. I am married now. Please go.

ONEGIN.

> I DON'T CARE
> I'M HOLDING FAST
> I BELIEVE MYSELF
> I BELIEVE MY BELL
> I WILL STAY THIS COURSE
> AND WAIT FOR YOU ALL DAYS
> LAY MY HEART OUT AS IT SURELY LAYS
> AT YOUR MARVELOUSLY PERFECT FEET.

TATYANA.

> OH GOD.

TATYANA & ONEGIN.

> DO WHAT YOU WILL
> DO WHAT YOU WILL
> DO WHAT YOU WILL WITH ME.

I WILL DIE, I WILL DIE
AS WE ALL MUST DIE.
I WILL DIE, I WILL DIE
AS WE ALL MUST DIE.
SO CLOSE, SO CLOSE, SO CLOSE!

TATYANA.

NO.
NO, TANYA, NO.
RETAIN SOME MEASURE OF CONTROL, TANYA, NO
YOU CANNOT HAVE THE PAST
MY FATE IS SET, I AM WED.
I AM TRUE TO HIM

ONEGIN.

NO, NO, NO.

TATYANA.

ENOUGH, ENOUGH!

ONEGIN.

NO, DO NOT GO

TATYANA.

ENOUGH, ENOUGH!

ONEGIN & TATYANA.

I LOVE YOU.

TATYANA.

I AM DECIDED

Goodbye.

> (**TATYANA** *leaves.*)
>
> (**ONEGIN** *looks around.*)

ONEGIN.

LOOK
OUTSIDE THE WINDOW
BIRCH TREES
A BIRD IN FLIGHT
TAKES A BRANCH
AND THEN ALOFT AGAIN
I WILL DIE, I WILL DIE
AS WE ALL MUST DIE

LET ME DIE, LET ME DIE
AS WE ALL MUST DIE
AT LAST THE LIGHT
AT LAST THE SUN
AT LAST MY HEART'S TRUE CRY
I LIVE,
I LIVE,
I LIVE

  *(***ONEGIN*** exits.)*

  *(***TATYANA*** appears.)*

TATYANA.
  LOOK AROUND, LOOK AROUND, LOOK AROUND
ALL.
  LOOK AROUND, LOOK AROUND, LOOK AROUND
TATYANA.
  IF I WANTED TO LIVE IN LOVE, IN LOVE
ONEGIN.
  A LOVE SONG I SING TO YOU

  (The **COMPANY** *emerges.)*

ALL.
  A LOVE SONG I SING TO YOU
  IT'S RUSSIA, IT'S WINTER, IT'S A LONG TIME AGO
  IF I WANTED TO LIVE IN LOVE, IN LOVE
  THEN YOU ARE WHOM I WOULD CHOOSE...

The End